WALT DISNEY'S
The Jungle Book

GROLIER
BOOK CLUB EDITION

It was a quiet day deep in the Indian jungle. Bagheera the panther was walking along the river. Suddenly the silence was broken by a strange sound. Bagheera went to see what was making the noise. It was a man-cub! He found the baby boy in a basket, which lay in a half-sunken boat.

Bagheera felt sorry for the baby. Carefully he
carried the basket ashore.

"The man-cub will never survive without a
mother," Bagheera said to himself. "What should
I do with you, little fellow?" he asked the smiling
baby.

Bagheera remembered that a wolf family lived
nearby. Perhaps they would adopt the man-cub.

Bagheera brought the basket to the wolves'
den. When the mother wolf and her cubs found
the laughing baby, they smiled. Rama, the father
wolf, was not so pleased at first. But soon he, too,
was smiling at the man-cub.

The wolves named the man-cub Mowgli. For ten years he lived happily in the jungle. Mowgli learned many things from the wolves.

He learned how to run like a wolf.

He learned how to scratch himself like a wolf.
He even learned how to play dead like a wolf,
just for fun!

But one day there was some bad news in the jungle. Shere Khan the tiger had returned. The fearsome tiger hated all humans because a hunter had once shot at him. Mowgli was now in danger! So late that night the wolf pack gathered with Bagheera on Council Rock.

"Even the strength of the pack is no match for Shere Khan," declared Akela, the pack leader. "The man-cub must leave at once."

"But he is like my own cub," protested Rama. "Where will he go?"

Then Bagheera spoke up. "Perhaps I can help. I know of a man-village where Mowgli will be safe. I will take him there."

It was agreed that Bagheera and Mowgli should leave the next morning. But taking Mowgli to the man-village would not be easy.

"*This* is my home," protested Mowgli as Bagheera tried to pry him from a tree. "I don't want to leave the jungle."

Reluctantly Mowgli began the journey to the
man-village with Bagheera. Night began to fall.
When they came to a big tree, Bagheera decided
they would spend the night there.

"Go to sleep," he told Mowgli as they settled
themselves on a large branch.

But they were not alone. Kaa the snake was hiding in the tree, and he thought Mowgli would make a tasty treat! "Yes, man-cub," Kaa whispered as he slithered down the tree, "go to sssleep."

Mowgli woke up and saw Kaa.
"Go away. Leave me alone,"
he said to the snake.

But Kaa just smiled an evil smile and said,
"Do not be afraid, man-cub. Trussst me. Go to
sssleep."

Kaa stared at Mowgli. Mowgli stared back, but
he began to feel dizzy. He was under Kaa's spell.
Kaa wrapped his long tail around Mowgli.

Bagheera woke up just in time! "What are you doing, Kaa?" he shouted. Bagheera slapped Kaa with his paw before the snake could hurt Mowgli. Kaa fell to the ground with a THUD!

"You have made a ssserious missstake, Bagheera," said Kaa as he slithered off.

Back up on the branch Bagheera said, "You see, Mowgli, the jungle is too dangerous for you. You will be safer in the man-village."

"But I want to live in the jungle. I can take care of myself," cried Mowgli.

"No," said Bagheera kindly. "You belong in the man-village. We will go there in the morning."

But Mowgli did not want to live in the man-village. So early the next morning, before Bagheera was awake, he ran away.

"I don't need anyone," Mowgli said to himself. But after a while he felt very lonely.

Then Mowgli heard somebody
singing.

"Dooby, dooby, doo, dooby, dooby, dee,"
sang Baloo, a big, friendly bear.

Baloo noticed Mowgli was by himself.
"Well, hello there, Little Britches," Baloo
said to him with a smile.

They quickly became friends.

"Will you teach me how to be a bear?" Mowgli asked.

"Sure!" Baloo answered.

So Baloo taught Mowgli how to dance like a bear and how to growl like a bear . . .

and even how to
fight like a bear!

"I want to stay in the jungle with you, Baloo,"
said Mowgli.

Later Baloo and Mowgli went for a swim. "I'll teach you all about the bare necessities of life, Mowgli," said Baloo as they floated down the river. "I like being a bear," Mowgli replied happily.

Neither of them noticed that several monkeys were watching them. The monkeys wanted to bring Mowgli to their leader, King Louie.

Before Baloo could stop them, the monkeys
grabbed Mowgli!

"Help me, Baloo!" cried Mowgli.

But the monkeys swiftly swung him around in
the treetops. Soon they were far from the river.
When the monkeys reached their home, they
brought Mowgli to King Louie.

"So you're the man-cub," said King Louie. "Crazy."

"I'm not crazy. You are!" said Mowgli.

"Have some bananas," said King Louie, shoving two into Mowgli's mouth.

"Tell you what," he continued. "I can fix it so that you can stay in the jungle. Have we got a deal?"

"Yes, sir," said Mowgli.

The monkeys decided to celebrate. Everybody started dancing.

Meanwhile Baloo had found the ancient ruins where the monkeys lived. In order to rescue Mowgli, he disguised himself as a big monkey and danced right into the party. Baloo made a very good monkey.

Baloo's plan worked. While the monkeys sang and danced, he carried Mowgli out of the ruins.

"Thanks for rescuing me," said Mowgli. "I didn't want to be a monkey. I would rather be a bear, like you."

"But you are *not* a bear, Mowgli," Baloo said sadly. "The jungle is too dangerous for you. You belong in the man-village."

"You are just like Bagheera!" shouted Mowgli. "I don't want to go to the man-village! I can take care of myself."

So Mowgli ran away from Baloo, too. He didn't even notice that a storm was approaching.

Mowgli ran through the jungle. Suddenly he ran right into Shere Khan! The tiger had been waiting for this moment. The man-cub was alone in the jungle at last.

"Do you know who I am, man-cub?" asked Shere Khan, showing the boy his sharp claws.

"Yes. But I am not afraid of you," said Mowgli.

"You must be afraid of me. Everyone is afraid of me," said Shere Khan smugly.

"Well, you don't scare me," said Mowgli.

"Ah, you have spirit for one so small," said the tiger. "You deserve a sporting chance. I will close my eyes and count to ten. It makes the chase

more interesting." Shere Khan began to count,
"One, two, three . . . "

But Mowgli did not run away. Instead he
reached for a stick.

Suddenly there was a loud clap of thunder. The storm had arrived.

Just as Shere Khan was about to attack
Mowgli, a bolt of lightning flashed in the sky.
The lightning hit a nearby tree, starting a fire.

Shere Khan let out a great roar. He was afraid
of fire!

Mowgli saw that Shere
Khan was afraid. He
picked up a burning branch
and chased the tiger away.
Soon the rain from the
storm put out the fire.

Just then Bagheera and
Baloo arrived together.
They both had been searching for Mowgli and
had heard Shere Khan's roar. They were happy to
see that Mowgli was not hurt.

"We're glad you're safe, Little Britches," said
Baloo as Mowgli ran up to the big bear and gave
him a happy hug.

"Baloo and I were very worried," added
Bagheera.

Mowgli hugged Bagheera, too, and told them
about his encounter with Shere Khan. By the
time he finished, the day was ending.

So the three
friends found
a safe place
to rest. Soon
they were all
fast asleep.

The following morning they all went to the
river near the man-village. When they arrived,
they heard someone singing. They crept closer.
A young girl was fetching some water from
the river.

"What's that?" asked Mowgli.

"That is a girl-cub," Bagheera told him.

Mowgli had never seen a girl-cub. He decided to take a closer look. As he approached her, he made a little noise. She turned and saw him. She smiled at Mowgli and dropped her jug of water.

"Hey, she did that on purpose," Baloo said as he and Bagheera watched from behind the bushes.

"Quite right, my friend," said the wise panther with a smile.

Mowgli quickly picked up the jug the young girl had dropped and refilled it with water. Then he followed her. Maybe he would like the man-village after all!

As Mowgli was about to enter the village, he smiled at his friends and waved good-bye.

"Well, Baloo," said Bagheera. "Mowgli will live in the man-village from now on. We will miss him, but he is where he belongs."

"Yes," agreed Baloo, "but I still think he would have made one swell bear."